THE
WUMP
WORLD

THE
WUMP
WORLD

written and illustrated by **BILL PEET**

HOUGHTON MIFFLIN COMPANY BOSTON

For my wife
MARGARET
who appreciates the marvels
of nature as much
as anyone

ISBN: 0-395-19841-0 REINFORCED EDITION
ISBN: 0-395-31129-2 SANDPIPER PAPERBOUND EDITION
PRINTED IN THE UNITED STATES OF AMERICA
WOZ 20 19 18 17 16 15

The Wump World was a small world, very much smaller than our world. There were no great oceans, lofty mountains, giant forests, or broad sandy deserts. The Wump World was mostly grassy meadows and clumps of leafy green trees with a few winding rivers and lakes. But it was perfect for the Wumps, who were the only creatures living there.

The Wumps were simple grass-eaters and spent most of their time grazing on the tall tender grass that grew in the meadows. In warm weather they cooled themselves in the crystal-clear rivers and lakes. And at night they slept in the shelter of the bumbershoot trees to keep the dew off their backs.

Since the Wumps had no enemies they wandered around just as they pleased with nothing whatever to worry about. However, the Wumps would have worried if they had known that someone a million miles away was watching their little world.

One morning the Wumps were awakened by a far-off humming sound. It seemed to be coming from somewhere above, and as the humming grew into a heavy roar, the sleepy-eyed Wumps crept through the trees for a peek at the sky.

Zooming straight for the earth came a great flock of potbellied monsters, with tails and fins, spitting fire and shooting out streaks of black smoke.

As the monsters swooped down to land, huge legs sprang from their bulging sides, and like gaping mouths doors flew open, then ramps shot to the ground. And down the ramps came a horde of tiny creatures swarming out onto the meadow.

These were the Pollutians from the planet Pollutus. They had left their worn-out old planet to start a new life in a new world. After such a long journey the Pollutians were overjoyed to find themselves on solid ground once more.

They were all prattling with excitement as they followed their leader, the topmost Pollutian and World Chief, across the meadow. At the top of a hill the chief stopped for a long look at the surrounding countryside.

Finally he said, "Looks good. We'll take it. Plant the flag, sergeant, and let's get things going!"

One shrill trumpet blast brought giant machines thundering out of the yawning spaceships, rolling down runways and out onto the meadow. The timid Wumps had been watching warily from the shelter of the trees, and at the sight of the giant machines they were horrified.

"Wump! wump!" they cried, and in a wild-eyed panic they went
humpity-clumping off through the trees to go diving headlong into
the nearest cave.

Then down they tumbled head over heels through a twisting tunnel to end up huddled together in dark caverns, while the earth-shaking machines rumbled and roared high above.

Once they got started, the monstrous machines moved at a furious pace, gobbling up trees and grinding them to bits.

More giant machines flattened the ground, followed by great scoopers and scrapers and diggers and gigantic cranes. Soon the entire Wump World was overrun.

The busy little Pollutians kept their mighty machines going full blast day and night without letup, in a frenzy to improve their wonderful new world.

Suddenly great cities sprang up. Huge factory buildings with towering smokestacks, high-rise apartment buildings and tall tall office buildings, and above them all loomed the hundred-story skyscrapers.

Along with the buildings came a tangle of streets and freeways with on ramps and off ramps, overpasses and underpasses, jammed with trucks and buses and cars of all sizes rushing pell-mell in every direction.

It was one great turmoil of noise and confusion and there was still
more to come.

Meanwhile the poor Wumps remained underground wandering aimlessly through the caverns feeding on the fuzzy green moss growing on the ledges and the mushrooms clustered in the crannies, and sipping the sweet water from pools fed by underground springs. But they were very unhappy. For all they knew, they might have to spend the rest of their days down there.

The Wumps didn't dare venture up to the surface, not even for a peek. They were much too frightened by the endless rumblings and roarings and loud screechings coming from above. And it was growing noisier by the day.

There was more and more noise and more of everything. More
buildings with more smokestacks puffing more and more smoke.

More freeways with more traffic shooting out more and more clouds of exhaust. More trash and more trash piles, with more and more waste gushing into the rivers and lakes.

Pretty soon the cities were so clouded by the factory smoke and
the fumes from the freeways the Pollutians could barely breathe.

They went sneezing and wheezing about the streets grouching and grumbling and blaming one another for the awful mess they were in.

One day an angry crowd gathered outside the World Tower building demanding to see the World Chief. When the chief appeared on his balcony all the Pollutians began shouting at once.

"We can't breathe the air! We can't drink the water! And we can't stand the noise! We've had enough!"

"Ah-ah-ker-choo!" sneezed the chief. "I know just how you feel. And something will be done at once. I promise."

With no time to lose the chief called for a meeting with his three top outer-spacemen.

"Gentlemen," he said, "this world of ours has gone sour. We've got to get out of here quick. But first we must find a new world. A better one. That's your job, men. So get going!"

"Righto, chief!" barked the men, and within fifteen minutes they were at the spaceport aboard their spaceships. Then *Zer-r-roosh! Zer-r-roosh! Zer-r-roosh!* the men took off in three directions, and in seconds they were zooming about in outer space at seven thousand miles an hour.

Days passed with no word from the outer-spacemen. After waiting a week the World Chief flew into a rage. "Blast it all," he bellowed, "what's keeping those blithering bubble heads?"

Then one Monday morning, out of the dark smudgy sky swooshed one of the spaceships.

As the ship touched down, the man hopped out shouting, "I've done it! I've done it! I've found a new world! A bigger and better world!"

"Nice going, lad!" cried the World Chief, and the crowd gathered at the spaceport gave their hero one great rousing cheer which ended in a fit of sneezing.

In no time the great news was sent flashing around the world over radio and TV warning all Pollutians to be packed and ready to go within twenty-four hours.

At dawn the next day the entire population swarmed into the
space center and crowded aboard the giant spaceships.

After double-checking to make sure all Pollutians were accounted for the World Chief gave the signal for blastoff. With a thunderous roar the giant ships shot off the ground *Ka-Zoom!* up and away through the smoke-blackened sky and were gone. And at long last peace and quiet settled over the Wump World.

The sudden silence came as a shock to the Wumps. They could hardly believe their ears. Still, they wanted to take no chances and so they remained in their caverns with ears cocked for the slightest sound.

After a long long silence they decided it was time to go, and, led by the biggest Wump, they crept up the tunnel to the cave entrance to find it covered by a crust of cement. With one powerful push of his snout the biggest Wump bumped his way through.

Then one by one the Wumps waddled out onto a freeway and gaped in wide-eyed amazement. They had feared something awful was happening to their world, but this was much more than they could have imagined.

They were staggered by the size of the huge buildings with walls and walls of windows looming up on every side, and the broad layers of hard, flat crust covering the earth which felt strangely cold to their feet. There was no sign of any tree or tuft of grass. Even the sky was gone. And the Wumps wondered if there was anything left for them. At least they must find out.

They wandered the freeways for miles only to find more and more buildings with endless heaps of wreckage and rubble. For all they could see their world was completely ruined. Footsore and weary, the Wumps were about to give up and head back for their cave when the biggest Wump let out a joyful "Wump!"

Just ahead of them was a grassy meadow with a clump of bumbershoot trees, all that was left of their lovely world. "Wump-wumping" for joy, the Wumps went bounding off the freeway out onto the meadow. Pretty soon the hungry Wumps were munching away on the tall tender grass. Now there was new hope for the Wumps.

In time the murky skies would clear up and the rains would wash the scum from the rivers and lakes. The tall buildings would come tumbling down and the freeways would crumble away. And in time the green growth would wind its way up through the rubble. But the Wump World would never be quite the same.